THE CHRONOLOGY PROTECTION CASE

Paul Levinson

Connected Editions

ISBN-13: 978-1-56178-056-3

First published as a novelette in Analog Magazine, September 1995

Finalist for the Nebula Award for best novelette of 1995

Reprinted in The Mammoth Book of Time Travel, 2013; The Best Time Travel Stories of All Time, 2003; Nebula Awards 32, 1998; Infinite Edge, 1997; Supernatural Sleuths, 1996

First story in the five-book Phil D'Amato series: The Chronology Protection Case (1995), The Copyright Notice Case (1996), The Silk Code (1999), The Consciousness Plague (2002), The Pixel Eye (2003)

Made into a movie by Jay Kensinger -- available FREE on Amazon Prime -- and a radio play by Mark Shanahan

Cover adapted from Jay Kensinger's poster for movie

Printed in the United States of America

Carl put the call through just as I was packing up for the day. "She says she's some kind of physicist," he said, and although I rarely took calls from the public, I jumped on this one.

"Dr. D'Amato?" she asked.

"Yes?"

"I saw you on television last week -- on that cable talk show. You said you had a passion for physics." Her voice had a breathy elegance.

"True," I said. Forensic science was my profession, but cutting edge physics was my love. Too bad there wasn't a way to nab rapist murderers with spectral traces. "And you're a physicist?" I asked.

"Oh yes, sorry," she said. "I should introduce myself. I'm Lauren Goldring. Do you know my work?"

"Ahm...," The name did sound familiar. I ran through the rolodex in my head, though these days my computer was becoming more reliable than my brain. "Yes!" I snapped my fingers. "You had an article in *Scientific American* last month about some Hubble data."

"That's right," she said, and I could hear her relax just a bit. "Look, I'm calling you about my husband -- he's disappeared. I haven't heard from him in two days."

"Oh," I said. "Well that's really not my department. I can connect you to--"

"No, please," she said. "It's not what you think. I'm sure his disappearance has something to do with his work. He's a physicist too."

***

I was in my car 40 minutes later on my way to her house, when I should have been home with pizza and the cat. No contest: a physicist in distress always wins.

Her Bronxville address wasn't too far from mine in Yonkers.

"Dr. D'Amato?" she opened the door.

I nodded. "Phil."

"Thank you so much for coming," she said, and ushered me in. Her eyes looked red, like she suffered from allergies or had been crying. But few people have allergies in March.

The house had a quiet appealing beauty. As did she.

"I know the usual expectations in these things," she said. "He has another woman, we've been fighting. And I'm sure that most women whose vanished husbands *have* been having affairs are quick to profess their certainty that that's not what's going on in *their* cases."

I smiled. "Ok, I'm willing to start with the assumption that your case is different. Tell me how."

"Would you like a drink, some wine?" she walked over to a cabinet, must've been turn of the century.

"Just ginger ale, if you have it," I said, leaning back in the plush Morris chair she'd shown me into.

She returned with the ginger ale, and some sort of sparkling water for herself. "Well, as I told you on the phone, Ian and I are physicists--"

"Is his last name Goldring, like yours?"

Lauren nodded. "And, well, I'm sure this has something to do with his project."

"You two don't do the same work?" I asked.

"No," she said. "My area's the cosmos at large -- big bang theory, black holes in space, the big picture. Ian's was, is, on the other end of the spectrum. Literally. His area's quantum mechanics." She started to sob.

"It's ok," I said. I got up and put my hand on her shoulder. Quantum mechanics could be frustrating, I knew, but not *that* bad.

"No," she said. "It isn't ok. Why am I using the past tense for Ian?"

"You think some harm's come to him?"

"I don't know," her lips quivered. She did know, or thought she knew.

"And you feel this has something to do with his work with tiny particles? Was he exposed to dangerous radiation?"

"No," she said. "That's not it. He was working on something called quantum signaling. He always told me everything about his work -- and I told him everything about mine -- we had that kind of relationship. And then a few months ago, he suddenly got silent. At first I thought maybe he *was* having an affair--"

And the thought popped into my head: if I had a woman with your class, an affair with someone else would be the last thing on my mind.

"But then I realized it was deeper than that. It was something, something that frightened him, in his work. Something that I think he wanted to shield me from."

"I'm pretty much of an amiable amateur when it comes to quantum mechanics," I said, "but I know something about it. Suppose you tell me all you know about Ian's work, and why it could be dangerous."

***

What I in fact fully grasped about quantum mechanics I could write on a postcard to my sister in Boston and it would likely fit. It had to do with light and particles so small that they were often indistinguishable in their behavior, and prone to paradox at every turn. A particularly vexing aspect that even Einstein and his colleagues tried to tackle in the 1930s involved two particles that at first collided and then travelled at sublight speeds in opposite directions: would observation of one have an instantaneous effect on the other? Did the two particles, having once collided, now exist ever after in some sort of mysterious relationship or field, a bond between them so potent that just to measure one was to influence the other, regardless of how far away? Einstein wondered about this in a thought experiment. Did interaction of subatomic particles tie their futures together forever, even if one stayed on Earth and the other wound up beyond Pluto? Real experiments in the 1960s and after suggested that's just what was happening, at least in local areas, and this supported Heisenberg's and Bohr's classic "Copenhagen" interpretation that quantum mechanics was some kind of mind-over-matter deal -- that just looking at a quantum or tiny particle, maybe even thinking about it, could affect not only it but related particles. Einstein would've preferred to find another cause -- non-mental --

for such phenomena. But that could lead to an interpretation of quantum mechanics as faster-than-light action -- the particle on Earth somehow sent an instant signal to the particle in space -- which of course ran counter to Einstein's relativity theories.

Well, I guess that would fill more than your average postcard. The truth is blood and semen and DNA evidence were a lot easier to make sense of than quantum mechanics, which was one reason that kind of esoteric science was just a hobby with me. Of course, one way that QM had it over forensics is that it rarely had to do with dead bodies. But Lauren Goldring was wanting to tell me that maybe it did in at least one case, her husband's.

"Ian was part of a small group of physicists working to demonstrate that QM was evidence of faster-than-light travel, time travel, maybe both," she said.

"Not a product of the mind?" I asked.

"No," she said, "not as in the traditional interpretation."

"But doesn't faster than light travel contradict Einstein?" I asked.

"Not necessarily," Lauren said. "It seems to contradict the simplest interpretations, but there may be some loopholes."

"Tell me more," I said.

"Well, there's a lot of disagreement even among the small group of people Ian was working with. Some think the data supports both faster than light *and* time travel. Others are sure that time travel is impossible even though--"

"You're not saying that you think some crazy envious scientist killed him?" I asked.

"No," Lauren said. "It's much deeper than that."

A favorite phrase of hers. "I don't understand," I said.

"Well, Stephen Hawking, for one, says that although the equations suggest that time travel might be possible on the quantum level, the universe wouldn't let this happen..." She paused and looked at me. "You've heard about Hawking's work in this area?"

"I know about Hawking in general," I said. "I'm not that much of an amateur. But not about his work in time travel."

"You're very unusual for a forensic scientist," she said, with an admiring edge I very much liked. "Anyway, Hawking thinks that whatever quantum mechanics may permit, the universe just won't allow time travel -- because the level of paradox time travel would create would just unravel the whole universe."

"You mean like if I could get a message back to JFK that he would be killed, and he believed me and acted upon that information and didn't go to Dallas and wasn't killed, this would create a world in which I would grow up with no knowledge that JFK had ever been killed, which would mean I would have no motive to send the message that saved JFK, but if I didn't send that message then JFK would be killed--"

"That's it," Lauren said. "Except on the quantum level you might achieve that paradox by sending back information just a few seconds in time -- say, in the form of a command that would shut down the generating circuit and prevent the information from being sent in the first place--"

"I see," I said.

"And, well, because things like that, if they could happen, if they happened all the time, would lead to a constantly remade, inside-out, self-effacing universe, Hawking promulgated his 'Chronology Protection Conjecture' -- the universe protects the existing time line, whatever the theoretical possibilities of time travel."

"How does your husband fit into this?" I asked.

"He was working on a device, an experiment, to disprove Hawking's conjecture," she said. "He was trying to create a local wormhole with temporal effects."

"And you think he somehow disappeared into this?" Jeez, this was beginning to sound like a bad episode of *Star Trek*. But she seemed rational, everything she'd outlined made sense, and something in her manner continued to compel my attention.

"I don't know," she looked like she was close to tears again.

"All right," I said. "Here's what I think we should do. I'm going to call in Ian's disappearance to a friend in the department. He's a precinct captain, and he'll take this seriously. He'll contact all the airports, get Ian's picture out to cops on the beat--"

"But I don't think--"

"I know," I said. "You've got a gut feeling that something more profound is going on. And maybe you're right. But we've got to cover all the bases."

"Ok," she said quietly, and I noticed that her lips were quivering again.

"Will you be ok tonight? I'll be back to you tomorrow morning." I took her hand.

"I guess so," she said huskily, and squeezed my hand.

I didn't feel like letting go, but I did.

***

The news the next morning was terrible. I don't care what the shrinks say: flat-out confirmed death is always worse than ambiguous, unresolved disappearance.

I couldn't bring myself to just call her on the phone. I drove to her home, hoping she was in.

She opened the door. I tried to keep a calm face, but I'm not that good an actor.

She understood immediately. "Oh no!" she cried out. She staggered and collapsed in my arms. "Please no."

"I'm sorry," I said, and touched her hair. I felt like kissing her forehead, but didn't. I hardly knew her, yet I felt very close to her, a part of her world. "They found him a few hours ago near Columbia University. Looks like another stupid, senseless, goddamned random drive-by shooting. That's the kind of world we live in." I didn't know whether this would in any way lessen her pain. At least his death had nothing to do with his work.

"No, not random," she said, sobbing. "Not random."

"Ok," I said, "you need to rest. I'm going to call someone over here to give you a sedative. I'll stay with you till then."

The medic arrived in 15 minutes. He gave her a shot, and she was asleep a few minutes later. "Not random. Not random," she mumbled.

I called the Captain, and asked if he could send a uniform over to stay with Lauren for the afternoon. He wasn't happy --

his people were overworked, like everyone -- but he owed me. Many's the time I'd saved his butt with some piece of evidence I'd uncovered in the back of an orifice.

I dropped by the autopsy. Nothing unusual there. Three bullets from a cheap punk's gun, one shattered the heart, did all the damage, Ian Goldring's dead. No sign of radiation damage, no strange chemistry in the body. No possible connection that I could see to anything Lauren had told me. Still, the coroner was a friend, I explained to him that the victim was the husband of a friend, and asked if he could run any and every conceivable test at his disposal to determine if there was anything different about this corpse. He said sure. I knew he wouldn't find anything though.

I went back to my office. I thought of calling Lauren and telling her about the autopsy, but she'd be better off if I let her rest. I was tired of looking at dead bodies. I turned on my computer and looked at its screen instead. I was on a few physics lists on the Internet. I logged on and did some reading about Hawking and his chronology protection conjecture.

"Lady physicist on the phone for you again," Carl called out. It was late afternoon already. I logged off and rubbed my eyes.

"Hi," Lauren said.

"You ok?" I asked.

"Yeah," she said. "I just got off the phone with one of the other researchers in Ian's group, and I think I've got part of this figured out." She sounded less tentative than yesterday -- like she was indeed more on top of what was actually going on, or thought she was -- but more worried.

I started to tell her, gently as I could, about the autopsy.

"Doesn't matter," she interrupted me. "I mean, I don't think the *way* that Ian was killed has any relevance to this. It's the fact that he *was* killed that counts -- the reason he was killed."

The reason -- everyone wants reasons in this irrational society. Science in the laboratory deals with reason. In the outside world, you're lucky if you can find a reason. "I know it's painful," I said. "But Ian's death had no reason -- his killer was likely just a high-flying kid with a gun. Happens all the time. Ian was just in the wrong place. A random victim in the murder lottery."

"No, not random," Lauren said.

She'd said the same thing this morning. I could hear her starting to sob again.

"Look, Phil," she continued. "I really think I'm close to understanding this. I'm going to make a few more calls. I, uh, we hardly know each other, but I feel good talking this out with you. Our conversation last night helped me a lot. Can I call you back in an hour? Or maybe -- I don't know, if you're not busy tonight -- could you come over again?"

She didn't have to ask twice. "I'll see you at seven. I'll also bring some food in case you're hungry -- you have to eat."

***

I knew even before I drove up that something was wrong. I guess my eyes after all these years of looking around crime scenes are especially sensitive to the weak flicker of police lights on the evening sky at a distance. The flicker still turns my stomach.

"What's going on here?" I got out of my car, Chinese food in hand, and asked the uniform.

"Who the hell are you?" he replied.

I fumbled for my ID.

"He's ok," Janny Murphy, the uniform who'd come to stay with Lauren in the afternoon, walked over. "He's forensics."

The food dropped from my hand when I saw the expression on her face. Brown moo-shoo pork juice dribbled down the driveway.

"It's crazy," Janny said. "Doc says it's less than one in ten thousand. Some rare allergy to the shot the medic gave her. It wasn't his fault. It somehow brings out an asthma attack hours later. Fifty percent fatality."

"And Lauren -- Dr. Goldring -- was in the unlucky part of the curve."

Janny nodded.

"I don't believe this," I said, shaking my head.

"I know," Janny said. "Helluva coincidence. Physicist and his wife, also a physicist, both dying like that."

"Maybe it's not a coincidence," I said.

"What do you mean?" Janny said.

"I don't know what I mean," I said. "Is Lauren -- is the body -- still here? I'd like to have a look at her."

"Help yourself," Janny gestured inside the house.

I can't say Lauren looked at peace in death. I could almost still see her lips quivering, straining to tell me something, though they were as sealed as the deadest night now. I had an urge again to kiss her face. I'd known her all of two days, wanted as many times to kiss her.

I was aware of Janny standing beside me.

"I'm going home now," I said.

"Sure," Janny said. "The Captain says he'd like to talk to you tomorrow morning. Just to wrap this whole mess up. Bad karma."

Yeah, karma, like in Fritz Capra's *Tao of Physics*. Like in two entities crossing each other's paths and then ever more touching each other's destinies. Like me and this soul with the soft, still lips. Except I had no power to influence Lauren, to make things better for her any more. And the truth is, I hadn't done much for her when she was alive.

***

I was awake all night. I logged on to a few more fringy physics lists and did more reading. Finally it was light outside. I thought about calling Stephen Hawking. He was where? California? Cambridge, England? I wasn't sure. I knew he'd have the capacity to talk to me if I could reach him -- he was fluent talking through that special device -- but he'd probably think I was crazy when I told him what I had to say. So I called Jack Donovan instead. He was another friend who owed me. I had lots of friends like that in the city. Jack was a science reporter for *Newsday*, and I'd come through for him with off-the-record background on murder investigations in my bailiwick lots of times. I hoped he'd come through for me now. I was starting to get worried. He had lots of connections in the field -- he could talk to scientists who'd shy away from me, my being in the Department and all.

It was seven in the morning. I expected to get his answering machine, but I got him. I told him my story.

"Ok," he said. "Why don't you go see the Captain at the precinct, and then come over to see me. I'll do some checking around in the meantime."

I did what Jack said. I kept strictly to the facts with the Captain -- no suppositions, no chronological or any other protection schemes -- and he took it all in with his customary frown. "Damn shame," he muttered. "Nice lady like that. They oughta take that sedative off the market. Damn drug companies are too greedy."

"Right," I said.

"You look exhausted," he said. "You oughta take the rest of the day off."

"More or less what I had in mind," I said, and left for Jack's.

***

I thought *my* office was high-tech, but Jack's Hempstead newsroom looked like something well into the next century. Wall-to-wall glimmering screens everywhere you looked, sounds of digital chirping like the patter of tiny raindrops.

Jack looked concerned. "You're not going to like this," he said.

"What else is new," I said. "Try me."

"Well, you were right about my having better entree to these physicists than you. I did a lot of checking," Jack said. "There were six people working actively in conjunction with Ian on this project. A few more, of course, if you take into account the usual complement of graduate student assistants. But outside of that, the project was sealed up pretty tightly -- not by the government or any agency, but by the researchers themselves. Sometimes they do that when the research gets really flakey -- like they don't want anyone to know what they're really doing until they're sure they have a reliable effect. You wouldn't believe some of the wild things people have been getting into in the past few years -- especially the physicists -- now that they have the Internet to constantly yammer at each other."

"I'm tired Jack. Please get to the point."

"Well, four of the seven -- that includes Ian Goldring -- are now dead. One had a heart attack -- the day after his doctor told him his cholesterol was in the bottom 10 percent. I guess that's not so strange. Another fell off his roof -- he was cleaning out his gutters -- and severed his carotid artery on a sharp piece of flagstone that was sticking up on his walkway. He bled to death before anyone found him. Another was struck by a car -- DOA. And then there's Ian. I could write a story on this even without your conjecture--"

"Please don't," I said.

"It's a weird situation all right. Four out of seven dying like that -- and also Goldring's wife."

"How are the spouses of the other fatalities?" I asked.

"All ok," Jack said. "But none are physicists. None knew anything at all about their husbands' work -- all of the dead were men. Lauren Goldring is the only one who had any idea what her husband was up to."

"She wasn't sure," I said. "But I think she figured it out just before she died."

"Maybe they all picked up some virus at a conference they attended -- something which threw off their sense of balance, caused their heart rate to speed up," Sam Abrahmson, Jack's editor, strolled by and jumped in. Clearly he'd been listening on the periphery of our conversation. "That could explain the two accidents and the heart attack," he added. "Maybe even the sedative death."

"But not the drive-by shooting of Goldring," I said.

"No," Abrahmson admitted. "But it could be an interesting story anyway. Think about it," he said to Jack and strolled away.

I looked at Jack. "Please, I'm begging you. If I'm right--"

"It's likely something completely different," Jack said. "Some completely different hidden variable."

Hidden variables. I'd been reading about them all night. "What about the other three? Have you been able to get in touch with them?" I asked.

"Nope," Jack said. "Hays and Strauss refused to talk to me about it. Both had their secretaries tell me they were aware of some of the deaths, had decided not to do any more work on the local wormhole project, had no plans to publish what they'd already done, didn't want to talk to me about it or hear from me again. Each claimed to be involved now in something completely different."

"Does that sound to you like the usual behavior of research scientists?" I asked.

"No," Jack said. "The ones I know eat up publicity, and they'd hang on to a project like this for decades, like a dog worrying a bone."

I nodded. "And the third physicist?"

"Fenwick? She's in a small plane somewhere in the outback of Australia. I couldn't reach her at all."

"Call me immediately if you hear the plane crashes," I said. I really meant "when" not "if," but I didn't want Jack to think I was even more far gone than I was. "Please try to hold off on any story for now," I said and made to leave.

"I'll do what I can," Jack said. "Try to get some rest. I definitely think there's something going on here all right, but not what you think."

***

The drive back to Westchester was harrowing. Two cars nearly sideswiped me, and one big-ass truck stopped so suddenly in front of me that I had all I could do to swerve out of crashing into it and becoming an instant Long Island Expressway pancake.

Let's say the QM time-travel people were right. Particles are able to influence each other travelling away from each other at huge distances, because they're actually travelling back in time to an earlier position when they were in immediate physical contact. So time travel on the quantum mechanical level is possible -- technically.

But let's say Hawking was also right. The universe can't allow time travel -- for to do so would unravel its very being. So it protects itself from dissemination of information backwards in time.

That wouldn't be so crazy. People are saying the universe can be considered one huge organism -- a Gaia writ large. Makes sense then, that this organism, like all other organisms, would have tendencies to act on behalf of its own survival -- would act to prevent its dissolution via time travel.

But how would such protection express itself? A physicist figures out a way of creating a local wormhole that can send some information back in time -- back to his earlier self and equipment -- in some non-blatantly paradoxical way. It doesn't shut off the circuit that sent it. So this information is in fact sent and in fact received -- by the scientist. But the universe can't allow that information transfer to stand. So what happens?

Hawking says the universe's first line of defense is to create energy disturbances severe enough at the mouths of the wormhole to destroy it and its time-channeling ability. Ok. But let's say the physicist is smart or lucky enough to create a wormhole that can withstand these self-disruptive forces? What does the universe do then?

Maybe it makes the scientist forget this information. Maybe causes a minor stroke in the scientist's brain. Maybe causes the equipment to irreparably break down. Maybe the lucky physicist is really unlucky. Maybe this already happened lots of times.

But what happens when a group of scientists around the world who achieve this time travel transfer reach a critical mass -- a mass that will soon publish its findings, and make them known, irrevocably, to the world?

Jeez! -- I jammed the heel of my hand into my car horn and swerved. The damn Volkswagen driver must be drunk out of his mind--

So what happens when this group of scientists gets information from its own future? Has proof of time travel, information that can't be? The universe regulates itself, polices its timeline, in a more drastic way. All existence is equilibrium -- a stronger threat to existence evokes a stronger reaction. A freak fatal accident. A sudden massive heart attack. Another no-motive, drive-by shooting that the universe already dishes out to all too many people in this hapless world of ours. Except in this case, the universe's motive is quite clear and strong: it must protect its chronology, conserve its current existence.

Maybe this already happened too. How many physicists on the

cutting edges of this science died too young in recent years? Jeez, here was a story for Jack all right.

But why Lauren? Why did she have to die?

Maybe because the universe's protection level went beyond just those who received illicit future information. Maybe it extended to those who understood just what it was doing, just--

Whamp! Something big had smashed into the rear of my car, and I was skidding way out of control towards the edge of the Throgs Neck Bridge, towards where some workers had removed the barriers to fix some corrosion or something. I was strangely calm, above it all. I told myself to go easy on the brakes, but my leg clamped down anyway and my speed increased. I wrenched my wheel around, but all that did was spin me into a backward skid off the bridge. My car sailed way the hell out over the black-and-blue Long Island Sound.

The way down took a long time. They'd say I was overwrought, over tired, that I lost control. But I knew the truth, knew exactly why this was happening. I knew too much, just like Lauren.

Or maybe there was a way out, a weird little corner of my brain piped up.

Maybe I didn't know the truth. Maybe I was wrong.

Maybe if I could convince myself of that, the universe wouldn't have to protect itself from me. Maybe it would give me a second chance.

My car hit the water.

I was still alive.

I was a pretty fair swimmer.

If only I could force myself never to think of certain things, maybe I had a shot.

Maybe the deaths of the physicists were coincidental after all...

I lost consciousness, thinking, no, I couldn't just forget what I already knew so well... How could I will myself not to think of that very thing I was trying to will myself not to think about ... that blared in my mind now like a broken car horn ... But if I died, what I knew wouldn't matter anyway...

***

I awoke fighting sheets ... of water. No, these were too white. Maybe hospital sheets. Yeah, white hospital sheets. They smelled like that too.

I opened my eyes. Hospital rooms were hell -- I knew better than most the truth of that -- but this was just a hospital room. I was sure of that. I was alive.

And I remembered everything. With a spasm that both energized and frightened me, I realized that I recalled everything I'd been thinking about the universe and its protective clutch...

But I was still alive.

So maybe my reasoning was not completely right...

"Dr. D'Amato," a female voice, soft but very much in command, said to me. "Good to see you awake."

"Good to *be* awake, Nurse, ah, Johnson," I squinted at her name tag, then her face. "Uhm, what's my situation? How long have I been here?"

She looked at the chart next to my bed. "Just a day and a half," she said. "They fished you out of the Sound. You were suffering from shock. Here," she gave me a cup of water. "Now that you're awake, you can take these orally." She gave me three pills, and turned off the intravenous that I'd just realized was attached to me. She disconnected the tubing from my vein.

I held the pills in my hand. I thought about the universe again. I envisioned it, rightly or wrongly, as a personal antagonist now. Let's say I was right about the reach of its chronology protection after all? Let's say it had spared me in the water, because I was on the verge of willing myself to forget? Let's say it had allowed me to get medicine and nutrition intravenously, while I was unconscious, because while

I was unconscious I posed no threat? But let's say now that I was awake, and remembered, it would--

"Dr. D'Amato. Are you falling back asleep on me?" She smiled. "Come on now, be a good boy and take your pills."

They burned in my palm. Maybe they were poison. Maybe something I had a lethal allergy to. Like Lauren. "No," I said. "I'm ok, now, really. I don't need them." I put the pills on the table, and swung my legs out of bed.

"I don't believe this," Johnson said. "It's true -- you doctors make the worst God-awful patients. You just stay put now -- hear me?" She gave me a look of exasperation and stalked out the door, likely to get the resident on duty, or, who knew, security.

I looked around for my clothes. They were on a chair, a dried out crumpled mess. They stank of oil and saltwater. At least my wallet was still inside my jacket pocket, money damp but intact. Good to see there was still some honesty left in this town.

I dressed quickly and opened the door. The corridor was clear. Goddamn it, I could leave if I wanted to. I was a patient not a prisoner.

At least insofar as the hospital was concerned. As for the larger realm of being, I couldn't say any more.

***

I took a cab straight home.

The most important new piece of evidence -- to this whole case, as well as to me personally -- was that I was alive. This meant that my assessment of the universe's vindictiveness was missing something. Or maybe the universe was just a less effective assassin of forensic scientists than quantum physicists and their knowing wives.

I called Jack to see if there was anything new.

"Oh, just a second please," the *Newsday* receptionist said. I didn't like the tone of her voice.

"Hello, can I help you?" This was a man's voice, but not Jack's. He sounded familiar but I couldn't place him.

"Yes, I'm Dr. Phil D'Amato of NYPD Forensics calling Jack Donovan."

Silence. Then, "Hello, Phil. I'm Sam Abrahmson. You still in the hospital?"

Right. Abrahmson. That was the voice. "No. I'm out. Where's Jack?"

Abrahmson cleared his throat. "He was killed with Dave Strauss this morning. He'd talked Strauss into going public with this -- Strauss supported your story. He'd picked Strauss up at his summer cottage in Ellenville -- Strauss had been hiding out there -- and was driving him back to the city. They got blown off a small bridge. Freak accident."

"No freakin' accident," I said. "You know that as well as I do." Another particle who'd danced this sick quantum twist with me. Another particle dead. But this one was completely my fault -- I'd brought Jack into this.

"I don't know what I know," Abrahmson said. "Except that at this point the story's on hold. Until we find out more."

I was glad to hear he sounded scared. "That's a good idea," I said. "I'll be back to you."

"Take care of yourself," Abrahmson said. "God knows what that subatomic radiation can do to the body and mind. Or maybe it's all just coincidence. God only knows. Take care of yourself."

"Right." Subatomic radiation. Abrahmson's latest culprit. First it was a virus, now it was radiation. I'd said the same stupid thing to Lauren, hadn't I. People like to latch on to something they know when faced with something they don't know -- especially something that kills some physicists here, a reporter there, who knew who else. But radiation had nothing to do with this. Stopping it would take a lot more than lead shields.

***

I tracked down Richard Hays. I was beginning to get a further inkling of what might be going on, and I needed to talk it out with one of the principals. One of the last remaining principals. It could save both our lives.

I used my NYPD clout to intimidate enough secretaries and assistants to get directly through to him.

"Look, I don't care if you're the bleeding head of the FBI," he said. He was British. "I'm going to talk to you about this just once, now, and then never again."

"Thank you, Doctor. So please tell me what you think is happening here. Then I'll tell you what I know, or think I know."

"What's happening is this," Hays said. "I was working on a project with my colleagues. That's true. But I came to realize the project was a dead-end -- that the phenomena we were investigating weren't real. So I ceased my involvement in that research. I have no intention of ever picking up that research again -- of ever publishing about it, or even talking about it, except to indicate that it was a waste of time. I'd strongly advise you to do the same."

I had no idea how he talked ordinarily, but his words on the phone sounded like each had been chosen with the utmost care. "Why do I feel like you're reading from a script, Dr. Hays?"

"I assure you everything I'm saying is real. As you no doubt already have evidence of yourself," Hays said.

"Now you look," I raised my voice. "You can't just sweep this under the rug. If the universe *is* at work here in some way, you think you can just avoid it by pretending you don't know about it? The universe would know about your pretense too -- it's after all still part of the universe. And word of this will get out anyway -- someone will sooner or later publish something. If you want to live, you've got to face this, find out what's really happening here, and--"

"I believe you are seriously mistaken, my friend. And that, I'm afraid, concludes our interview, now and forever." He hung up.

I held on to the disconnected phone, which beeped like a seal, for a long time. I realized that the left side of my body hurt, from my chest up through my shoulder and down my arm. The pain had come on, I thought, at the end of my futile lecture to Hays. Right when I'd talked about publishing. Maybe publishing was the key -- maybe talk about dissemination of this information, as opposed to just thinking about it, is what triggered the universe's backlash. But I was also sure I was right in what I'd said to Hays about the need to confront this, about not running away...

I put the phone back in its receiver and lay down. I was bone tired. Maybe I was getting a heart attack, maybe I wasn't. Maybe I was still in shock from my dip in the Sound. I couldn't fight this all on my own much longer.

***

The phone rang. I fumbled with the receiver. How long had I been sleeping? "Hello?"

"Dr. D'Amato?" a female voice, maybe Lauren's, maybe Nurse Johnson's. No, someone else.

"Yes?"

"I'm Jennifer Fenwick."

Fenwick, Fenwick -- yes, Jennifer Fenwick, the last quantum physicist on this project. I'd wheedled her number from Abrahmson's secretary and left a message for her in Australia -- the girl at the hotel wasn't sure if she'd already left. "Dr. Fenwick, I'm glad you called. I, uhm, had some ideas I wanted to talk to you about --regarding the quantum signaling project." I wasn't sure how much she knew, and didn't want to scare her off.

She laughed, oddly. "Well, I'm wide open for ideas. I'll take help wherever I can get it. I'm the only damn person left alive from our research group."

"Only person?" So she knew -- apparently more than I.

I looked at the clock. It was tomorrow morning already -- I'd slept right through the afternoon and night. Good thing I'd called my office and gotten the week off, the absurd part of me that kept track of such trivia noted.

"Richard Hays committed suicide last night," Fenwick's voice cracked. "He left a note saying he couldn't pull it off any longer -- couldn't surmount the paradox of deliberately not thinking of something -- couldn't overcome his lifelong urge as a scientist to tell the world what he'd discovered. He'd prepared a paper for publication -- begged his wife to have it published posthumously if he didn't make it. I spoke to her this morning. I told her to destroy it. And the note, too. Fortunately for her, she had no idea what the paper was about. She's a simple woman -- Richard didn't marry her for her brains."

"I see," I said slowly. "Where are you now?"

"I'm in New York," she said. "I wanted to come home -- I didn't want to die in Australia."

"Look, you're still alive," I said. "That means you've still got a chance. How about meeting me for lunch" -- I looked at the clock again -- "in about an hour. The Tratoria Il Bambino on 12th Street in the Village is good. As far as I know, no one there has died from the food as yet." How I could bring myself to make a crack like that at a time like this, I didn't know.

"Ok," Fenwick said.

***

She was waiting for me when I arrived. On the way down, I'd fantasized that she'd look just like Lauren. But in fact she looked a little older and wiser. And even more frightened.

"All right," I said after we'd ordered and gotten rid of the waiter. "Here's what I have in mind. You tell me as a physicist where this might not add up. First, everyone who's attempted to publish something about your work has died."

Jennifer nodded. "I spoke to Lauren Goldring the afternoon she died. She told me she was going to the press."

I sighed. "I didn't know that -- but it supports my point. In fact, the two times I even toyed with going public about this, I had fleeting interviews with death. The first time in the water, the second with some sort of pre-heart attack, I'm sure."

Jennifer nodded again. "Same for me. Wheeler wrote about cosmic censorship. Maybe he was on to the same thing as Hawking."

"All right, so what does that tell us?" I said. "Even thinking about publishing this is dangerous. But apparently it's not a capital offense -- knowing about this is in itself not fatal. We're still alive. It's as if the universe allows private knowledge in this area. It probably also allows public crackpot knowledge -- because no one takes crackpots seriously, even scientific ones. It's the danger of public dissemination by reliable sources that draws the response -- the threat of an objectively accepted scientific theory. So our private knowledge, yours and mine, isn't the real problem here. Communication is. The definite intention to publish. That's what kills you. Yeah, cosmic censorship is a good way of putting it."

"Ok," Jennifer said.

"Ok," I said. "But it's also clear that we can't just ignore this -- can't expect to suppress it in our minds. Not having any particular plan to publish won't be enough to save us -- not in the long run.

Sooner or later after a dark silent night we'd get the urge to shout it out. It's human nature. It's inside of us. Hays' suicide proves it -- his note spells it out. You can't just not think of something. You can't just will an idea into oblivion. It's self-defeating. It makes you want to get up on the rooftop and scream it to the world even more -- like a repressed love."

"Agreed," Jennifer said. "So what do we do, then?"

"Well, we can't go public with this story, and we can't will ourselves to forget it. But maybe there's a third way. Here's what I was thinking. I can tell you -- in strict confidence -- that we sometimes do this in forensics." I lowered my voice. "Let's say we have someone who was killed in a certain way, but we don't want the murderer to know that we know how the murder took place. We just deliberately at first publicly interpret the evidence in a different, false way – to the throw the murderer off. After all, there's usually more than one trauma that can result in a given fatal injury to a body -- more than one plausible explanation of how someone was killed. Slipped and hit your head on a rock, or someone hit you in the head with a rock -- sometimes there's not much difference between the results of the two."

"The universe is murderous, all right, I can see that, but I don't see how what you're saying would work in our situation," Jennifer said.

"Well, you tell me," I said. "Your group thinks it built a wormhole that allows signaling through time. But couldn't you find another phenomenon to attribute those effects to? After all, we only have time travel on the brain because of H. G. Wells and his literary offspring. Let's say Wells had never written *The Time Machine*? Let's say science fiction had taken a different turn? Then your group would likely have come up with another explanation for your findings. And you can do this now anyway!" I took a sip of wine and realized I felt pretty good. "You can publish an article on your work, and attribute your findings to something other than time travel. Indicate they're some sort of other physical effect. Come up with the equivalent of a bogus phlogiston theory, an attractively deceptive conception for this tiny sliver of subatomic phenomena, to account for the time travel effects. The truth is, few if any serious scientists actually believe that time travel is possible anyway, right? Most think it's just science fiction, nothing else. Who would have reason to suspect a time travel effect here unless you specifically called attention to it?"

Jennifer considered. "The graduate research assistants worked only on the data acquisition level. Only the project principals, the seven of us," she caught her breath, winced -- "only the seven of us knew this was about time travel. No one else. Ours were supposedly the best minds in this area. Lot of good it did us."

"I know," I tried to be as reassuring as I could. "But then without that time travel label, all you've got is another of a hundred little experiments in this area per year -- I checked the literature, there actually are a lot more than that -- and your study would likely get lost in the wash. That should shut the universe up. That should keep it safe from time travel -- send the scientific community off on the wrong track, in a different direction -- maybe not send them off in any direction all. Could you do that?"

Jennifer sipped her wine slowly. Her glass was shaking. Her lips clung to the rim. She was no doubt thinking that her life depended on what she decided to do now. She was probably right. Mine too.

"Exotic matter is what makes the effect possible," she said at last. "Exotic matter keeps the wormhole open long enough. No one knows much about how it works -- in fact, as far as I know, our group created this kind of exotic matter, in which weak forces are suspended, for the first time in our project. I guess I could make a case that a peculiar property of this exotic matter is that it creates effects that mimic time travel in artificial wormholes -- I could make a persuasive argument that we didn't really see time travel through that wormhole at all, what we have instead is a reversal of processes to earlier stages when they come in contact with our exotic matter, no signaling from the future. You know -- we thought the glass was half full, but it was really half empty."

"No," I said. "That's still not going far enough. You've got to be more daring in your deception -- come up with something that doesn't invoke time travel at all, even in the negative. Publishing a paper with results that are explicitly said not to demonstrate time travel is akin to someone the police never heard of coming into the station and saying he didn't do it -- that only arouses our suspicion. I'm sorry to be so blunt, Jennifer. But you've got to lie more blatantly. Can't you come up with some effects of exotic matter that have nothing to do with time travel at all?"

She drained her wine glass and put it down, neither half full nor half empty. Completely empty. "This goes against everything in my life and training as a scientist," she said. "I'm supposed to pursue the truth, wherever it takes me."

"Right," I said. "And how much truth will you be able to pursue when you're like Hays and Strauss and the others?"

"Einstein said the universe wasn't malicious," she said. "This is unbelievable."

"Maybe Einstein was saying the glass was half empty when he knew it was half full. Maybe he knew just what he was doing -- knew which side his bread was buttered on -- maybe he wanted to live past middle age."

"God Almighty!" She slammed her hand on the table. Glasses rattled. "Couldn't I just swear before you and the universe never to publish anything about this? Wouldn't that be enough?"

"Maybe, maybe not," I said. "From the universe's point of view, your publishing a paper that explicitly attributes the effects to something other than time travel might be much safer -- to you as well as the universe. Let's say you change your mind, years from now, and try to publish a paper that says you succeeded with time travel after all. You'd already be on record in the literature as attributing those effects to something else -- you'd be much less likely to be believed then. Better for the universe. Better for you. A paper with a false lead is not only our best bet now, it's an insurance policy for our future."

Jennifer nodded, very slowly. "I guess I could come up with something -- some phenomenon unrelated to time travel -- unsuggestive of it. The connection of quantum effects to human thought has always had great appeal, and even though I personally never saw much more than wishful thinking in that direction."

"Good," I said quietly and nodded.

"But how can we be sure no one else will want to look into these effects?" Jennifer asked.

I shrugged. "Guarantees of anything are beyond us in this situation. The best we can hope for are probabilities -- that's how the QM realm operates anyway, isn't it -- likelihoods of our success, statistics in favor of our survival. As for your effects, well, effects don't have much impact outside of a supportive context of theory. Psalm 51 says 'Cleanse me with hyssop and I shall be clean' -- and the penicillin mold was first identified on a piece of decayed hyssop by a Swedish chemist -- but none of this led to antibiotics until spores from a mold landed in Fleming's petri dish, and he placed them in the right scientific perspective. Scientists thought they had evidence of spontaneous generation of maggots in old meat, until they learned how maggots make love. Astronomers saw lots of evidence for a luminiferous ether, until Michelson-Morley decisively proved that wrong. You're working on the cutting edge of physics with your wormholes. No one knows what to expect -- you said it yourself -- yours were the best minds in this area. *You* can create the context. No one's left to contradict you. Let's face it, if you word your paper properly, it will likely go unnoticed. But if not, it will point people in the wrong direction -- and once pointed that way, away from time travel, the world could take years, decades, longer, to look at time travel as a real scientific possibility again. The history of science is filled with wrong glittering paths, tenaciously taken and defended. That's the path of life for us. I'm not happy about it, but there it is."

Our food arrived. Jennifer looked away from me, and down at her veal.

I hadn't completely won her over yet. But she'd stopped objecting. I understood how she felt. To theoretical scientists, pursuit of truth was sometimes more important than life itself. Maybe that's why I went into flesh-and-blood forensics. I pushed on. "The truth is, we've all been getting along quite well without time travel anyway -- it could wreak far more havoc in everyone's lives than nuclear weapons ever did. The universe may not be wrong here."

She looked up at me.

"It's all up to you now," I said. "I'm not a physicist. I can't pull this off. I can take care of the general media, but not the scientific journals." I thought about Abrahmson at *Newsday*. He hadn't a clue which way was up in this thing. He'd just as soon believe this nightmare was all coincidence -- the ever popular placeholder for things people didn't want to understand. I could easily pitch it to him in that way.

She gave me a weak smile. "Ok, I'll try it. I'll write the article with the mental spin on the exotic effects. *Physics Review D* was given some general info that we were doing something on exotic matter, and is waiting for our report. It'll have maximum impact on other physicists there. The human mind in control of matter will be catnip for a lot them anyway."

"Good," I smiled back. I knew she meant it. I knew because I suddenly felt very hungry, and dug into my own veal with a zest I hadn't felt for anything in a while. It tasted great.

Two particles of humanity had connected again. Maybe this time the relationship would go somewhere.

It occurred to me, as I took Jennifer's hand and squeezed it with relief, that maybe this was just what the universe had wanted all along.

As they say in the Department, an ongoing string of deaths is a poor way to keep a secret.

About the Author

Paul Levinson, PhD, is Professor of Communication & Media Studies at Fordham University in NYC. His nonfiction books, including *The Soft Edge* (1997), *Digital McLuhan* (1999), *Realspace* (2003), *Cellphone* (2004), and *New New Media* (2009; 2nd edition, 2012), have been translated into fifteen languages. His science fiction novels include *The Silk Code* (winner of Locus Award for Best First Science Fiction Novel of 1999), *Borrowed Tides* (2001), *The Consciousness Plague* (2002), *The Pixel Eye* (2003), *The Plot To Save Socrates* (2006), *Unburning Alexandria* (2013), and *Chronica* (2014) - the last three of which are also known as the Sierra Waters trilogy, and are historical as well as science fiction. He appears on CNN, MSNBC, Fox News, the Discovery Channel, National Geographic, the History Channel, NPR, and numerous TV and radio programs. His 1972 LP, *Twice Upon a Rhyme*, was re-issued in 2010. He reviews television in his InfiniteRegress.tv blog, and was listed in The Chronicle of Higher Education's "Top 10 Academic Twitterers" in 2009.

###

Phil D'Amato's adventures continue in *The Copyright Notice Case*, *The Silk Code*, *The Consciousness Plague*, and *The Pixel Eye*.

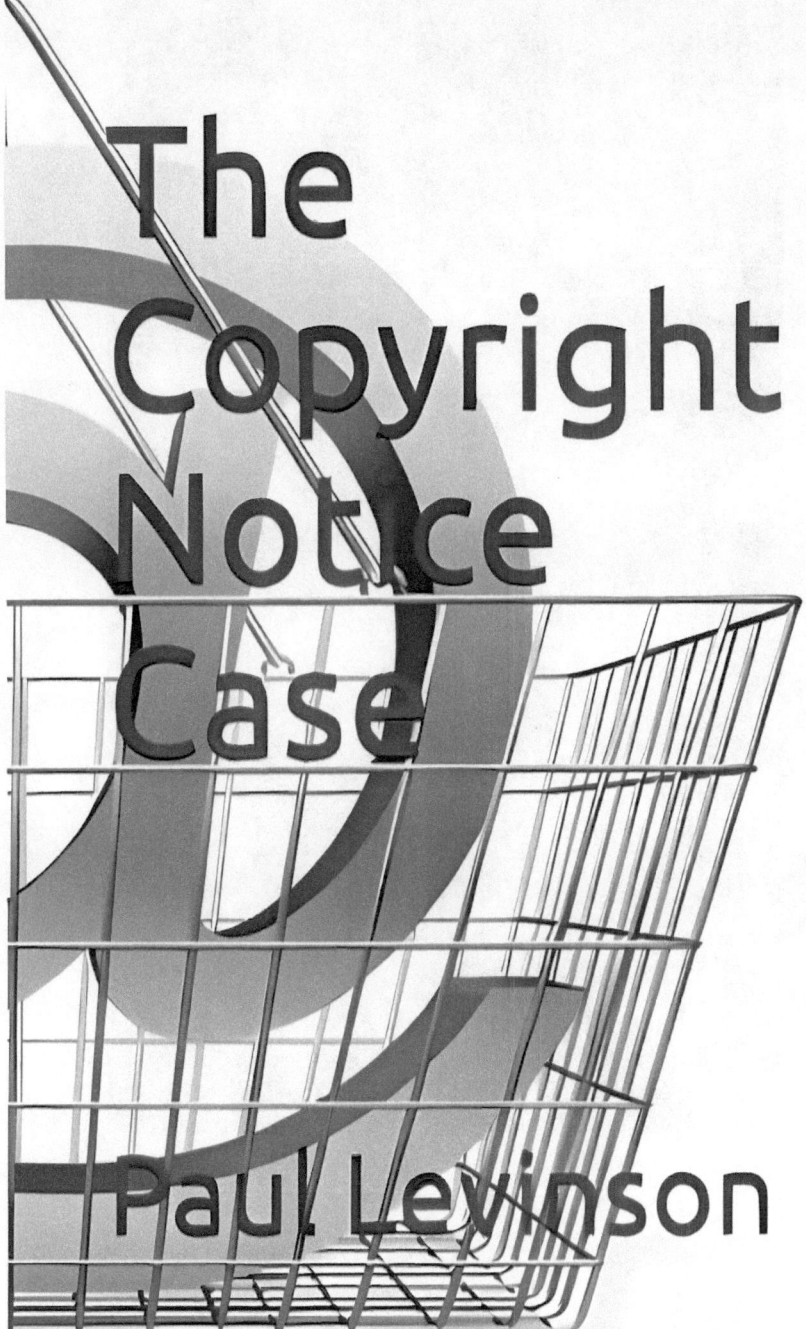

The Copyright Notice Case

Paul Levinson

THE

CONSCIOUSNESS PLAGUE

PAUL LEVINSON

"more nearly reaches the heights
of Isaac Asimov's classic sf
mysteries than most other genre
novels these days"

- Roland Green, Booklist

THE PIXEL EYE

PAUL LEVINSON

"The nuttiness of the premise and the grittiness of the near-future

New York ambiance are equally appealing" - NY Times

The following books by Paul Levinson available in print and Kindle:

Nonfiction:

The Soft Edge: A Natural History and Future of the Information Revolution

Digital McLuhan: A Guide to the Information Millennium

McLuhan in an Age of Social Media

Realspace: The Fate of Physical Presence in the Digital Age, On and Off Planet

New New Media

Fake News in Real Context

Science fiction:

Loose Ends (time travel) series (complete):
Loose Ends, Little Differences, Late Lessons, Last Calls

Sierra Waters (time travel) series:
The Plot to Save Socrates, Unburning Alexandria, Chronica

Phil D'Amato forensic detective series:
The Chronology Protection Case, The Copyright Notice Case, The Silk Code, The *Consciousness Plague, The Pixel Eye*

Ian's Ions and Eons (three time travel novelettes)

Exo-Genetic Engineers series:
The Orchard, The Suspended Fourth

Borrowed Tides

Double Realities series:
The Other Car, Extra Credit, The Wallet, The P&A

The Kid in the Video Store

PAUL LEVINSON

Nonfiction and Science Fiction

Touching the Face of the Cosmos: On the Intersection of Space Travel and Religion